T0209595

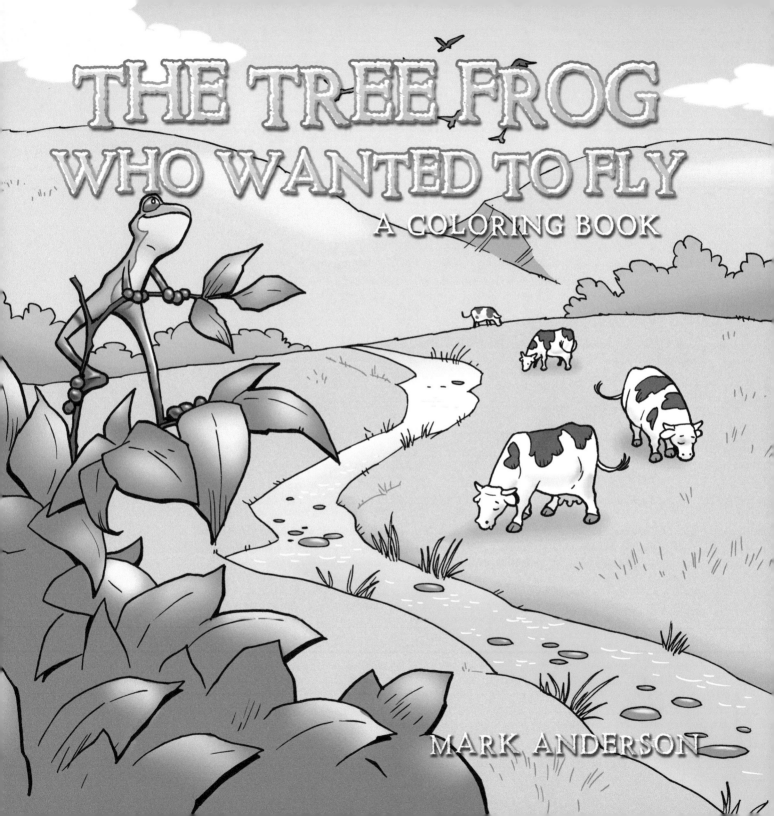

AuthorHouse™
1663 Liberty Drive
Bloomington, IN 47403
www.authorhouse.com
Phone: 1 (800) 839-8640

© 2019 Mark Anderson. All rights reserved.

No part of this book may be reproduced, stored in a retrieval system,
or transmitted by any means without the written permission of the author.

Published by AuthorHouse 07/15/2019

ISBN: 978-1-7283-1916-2 (sc)
ISBN: 978-1-7283-1917-9 (e)

Print information available on the last page.

This book is printed on acid-free paper.

Because of the dynamic nature of the Internet, any web addresses or links contained in this book may have changed
since publication and may no longer be valid. The views expressed in this work are solely those of the author and do not
necessarily reflect the views of the publisher, and the publisher hereby disclaims any responsibility for them.

authorHOUSE®

THE TREE FROG
WHO WANTED TO FLY

To Joan for our forty-odd years of friendship

A tree frog I met, and I swear this is true, he told me this
story, now I'm telling you.
It seems the young tree frog had one fondest wish
"I'm tired of life in this pond with the fish.
If I were a bird then I really could fly
and the next time we meet I'll be soaring up high
I just have to fly, to see what lies beyond
the cattails and duckweeds I see in my pond.
I could fly over fields and highways and rivers.
Just thinking about it still gives me the shivers.
I'd fly to the moon and give Luna a kiss
No, I really can't stand being grounded like this"

4

I'm a lot like a bird. I can perch in a tree
the same bugs that birds eat are tasty to me.
When I open my mouth and sing out yoo-hoo
I sound like a bird. At least I think I do.
We have so much in common, those fliers and I
so it's natural I ought to be able to fly."

But a sound from above made him flinch several flinches.
The laughter of grackles and blue jays and finches.
"To fly, Mr frog, you need several things
And two of those things are, you've got to have wings"
"Two wings are best a left and right
Flap them together to make the best flight"
"I think without wings to pull you around
The only direction that you'll fly is down!"
"Haven't you noticed that all flying creatures
Are endowed by nature with these standard features?
Dragon flies, bats, crows and macaws,
the weird flying monkeys from Wizard of Oz
We all have these wings to hold us aloft"
"Besides you're too fat", a young chickadee scoffed.
Then away they all flew to the upper O-zone
And the frog green with envy was left all alone.

8

Next morning early Frog made the decision
today he would fly despite their derision.
He mounted the tree in a positive mood
And he climbed and he climbed just as high he could.
The view of the wide world stirred up his blood
Then he looked down below at the pond and the mud.
He took a deep breath and he counted to ten
and he leapt into space and .. what happened then?
I suppose you could say that he sort of flew
He hung in the air for a second or two.

But that was just cause his leap was so strong
that first maiden flight didn't last very long.
Though his heart was elated, gravity frowned!
As the birds had predicted he could only fly down
Instead of the rapturous vast blue beyond
he landed kerspash in the green mucky pond.

12

As he sank to the bottom, his spirits did too
And for quite a long time didn't know what to do
"I wish I could I vanish and not leave a trace
Rather than rising and having to face
Those obnoxious birds who are waiting up there"
But even a frog will soon run out of air

He rose to the surface, confronting his fears
He knocked all the pond water out of his ears
He swam to the bank and looked all around
But what was he hearing? What is that sound?
The words that he heard from the birds were not jeering
Contrariwise they sounded like cheering
"Dude that was awesome the way you stayed down
on the floor of the pond so long!"
"We thought you drowned!"
"And then how you swam to the bank was amaze-ful
We had no idea that frogs were so graceful!"
"Tell us some stories, tell us how tell us where"
"Who else lives in the bog?"
"We've never been there".

Through his surprise the frog told a few tales
of catfish and crawdads and turtles and snails
Then swam on his back and he spouted like whales.
He made up a brag that he's swam the Caribbean
An impossible task for a freshwater amphibian

When he casually flicked out his tongue and ensnared
a passing cicada the birds only stared
in sheer admiration. Who would have thought?
Then they had tea and cookies that someone had brought.
And they mingled and chatted and talked quite a lot
about things they could do and things they could not.
The birds gave him lots of good flying advice and
Frog had to admit his new friends were quite nice.
They shared hugs and handshakes and promised "We'll see
You the next time you climb up in our locust tree"

When his friends had all flown and frog sat reflecting
he thought "well, that wasn't what I was expecting.
I've thought it all through and I have to confess
Swimming is kinda like flying I guess.
And making new friends is important, too.
Friends who encourage the things that you do.
Those things I learned from my embarrassing fall.
I still wish I could fly."

But then, don'wt we all?

Printed in the United States
By Bookmasters